LET'S GO TO THE
LIBRARY

by LISL WEIL

Holiday House/New York

Printed in the United States of America
FIRST EDITION

Library of Congress Cataloging-in-Publication Data

Weil, Lisl.
Let's go to the library / Lisl Weil.
p. cm.
Summary: Discusses the history of libraries, the effects of the invention of the printing press on them, what goes on in libraries, and some prominent libraries of the world.
ISBN 0-8234-0829-9
1. Libraries—Juvenile literature. [1. Libraries.] I. Title.
Z665.5.W45 1990
027—dc20 90-55105 CIP AC
ISBN 0-8234-0829-9

LET'S GO TO THE
LIBRARY

Books are good friends. They can be held and hugged. They can be carried to the beach or to school. They can be filled with make-believe stories or with true tales, and they can teach.

With a book, one can travel far while sitting still.

Books open windows and doors to the exciting world of the past, the present, and the future. Very few people own all the books they would like to read. But they can go to the library, where they will never run out of choices.

The library is filled with books for people of all ages. In fact, the word *library* comes from the Latin word *liber,* which means book.

The library is a friendly place where people can settle down and read to their heart's content. They can also look up answers to questions in dictionaries and encyclopedias.

Most public libraries have a special section for children. Not only is it filled with wonderful books, but it has toys, records, tapes, and videos, too. Children can enjoy programs designed just for them. One of the most popular is story hour, during which the librarian reads a picture book or tells a story.

Libraries usually have study spaces set aside for people working on a project. They can do research by looking up information on microfilm and microfiche—films of printed information—or by using one of the library's computers.

They can make copies of their research on the copy machine and send messages on the library's fax machine.

A library lends books to people wanting to read or study at home.

One can also go to the library to hear lectures and watch movies, videos, or slides.

A library provides records or tapes, too, and even programs for meeting famous authors.

A library often has an exhibit of photographs, paintings, or old books. Sometimes, although rarely, it even has a store for selling books.

Many trained and learned people make a library run smoothly, but the most important person is the librarian.

There are many different kinds of librarians.

Some have been trained as reference librarians. They help people who are doing research.

Others have been trained as children's librarians. They buy books that they think young people will enjoy, and they plan programs for children.

And there are adult librarians who build collections of books for older readers.

But all librarians have one thing in common. They have studied at library school, where they received a degree in Library and Information Science. Nowadays, many graduate with the title of media specialist. A media specialist is really a modern name for a librarian. The new term shows that librarians are responsible for more than just books. They know about computers, films and other "media" too.

Besides a librarian or media specialist, a library needs a director or president to make its important decisions and run the library. There must also be cataloguers—trained people who arrange the materials in a library in a way that makes them easy to use. They assign a number to a book that shows where it can be found in the stacks or on the shelves. There are also people who are in charge of replacing books that are in bad condition. And there are staff members who plan special exhibits and events or raise money and receive donations. Besides paid staff members, libraries depend on people who like to help. They are called volunteers.

At small libraries, a few people share all the work that needs to be done.

The grand New York Public Library at Fifth Avenue and 42nd Street

There are many kinds of libraries in America.

The public library is financed by local and federal tax money as well as by donations. People can go into the stacks to find books. Public libraries are sometimes open on Sundays and at least one week-night, as well as on weekdays.

There are public bookmobiles that travel to places that have no libraries. A large van or bus carries the books and a librarian travels with them.

There are tiny public lending libraries that are located in rural kitchens or grocery stores.

And there are public libraries that address special interests: music, film, theater, television, dance, science, law, sports, and more.

Blind people have their own sections in some libraries filled with books written in braille. Blind people read braille with their fingertips and listen to tapes and records at the library, too.

Besides public libraries, there are school and university libraries created for the use of students. They are financed by tax money or by private funds.

Libraries, like the Morgan Library in New York City, are private. They are financed only by wealthy individuals. One such individual was Andrew Carnegie, the son of a Scottish immigrant. After making millions of dollars in the steel business, he gave money for 2,800 libraries to be built in America and the United Kingdom.

Nowadays, we take libraries for granted. But they were not always the way they are today. Perhaps the idea of collecting written material started with prehistoric man, who scratched messages and warning signs on rocks and stones, then saved them.

The ancient Egyptians of royal birth wrote stories about their triumphs on ivory tablets. We have discovered fine temple collections from the reign of King Ramses in 1200 B.C.—about 3,000 years ago.

In Nineveh, the ancient Assyrian capital, there was a palace collection in the first century B.C. that held more than 20,000 tablets, all arranged neatly in jars.

The first library that was a public place of reading was the Library of Alexandria, a city in Egypt. Founded by Ptolemy Soter in about 280 B.C., it was filled with Greek plays and literature as well as several thousand papyrus scrolls.

By then, people were using a rough kind of paper discovered by the Egyptians. Made from the reed of the papyrus plant, each roll could be stored in a jar on a shelf or in a hole in a library wall.

Ancient Greece had many libraries right up through the third century A.D. Not only were they connected to temples and schools, but famous thinkers like Aristotle and Plato had large private collections, too.

The libraries of ancient Rome were filled with the works of the Greeks whom the Romans conquered from 200 B.C. until the third century A.D. They brought back books as spoils of war. Wealthy Roman families also had large private collections.

The first Christian libraries grew up in the fourth century as a means of saving the words of Jesus, the early gospels, and other scriptures. The Imperial Library, founded by Constantine the Great in Constantinople in about 350 A.D., was famous throughout the world. In Europe, from the sixth through the fifteenth centuries, monks and missionaries created beautiful hand-lettered, illustrated manuscripts for their churches and kings. Monasteries and cathedral libraries contained many of these handmade books.

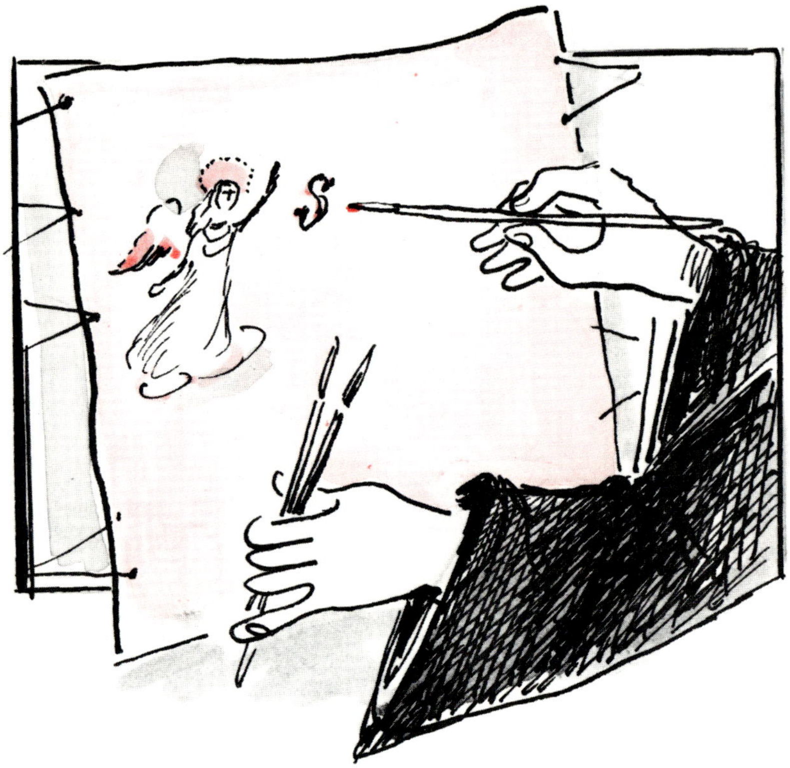

The monks used a material called parchment. It was made from the dried and pressed skin of sheep and goats. Sometimes, they also wrote on thin pieces of leather. Today, we still use parchment for diplomas and other special documents.

Paper was introduced by the Chinese, who invented it in the first century. It spread to Japan in A.D. 600. It came to the Middle East via central Asia in 800 A.D. Made from linen or cotton rags, it was used for writing down the Moslems' sacred book, the Koran. Paper mills in Italy were set up in the 1300s to make paper for handmade "books" that were then stored in libraries. A major change in the way libraries were set up came after movable type was invented in 1457 by a German printer named Johann Gutenberg.

His type was set by hand and printed on handmade paper. The first printed book became known as the Gutenberg or Mazarin Bible. It was kept in the library of Cardinal Mazarin in Paris, France.

After type was invented, books were printed and placed in libraries all over Europe. The largest and most important library in the fifteenth century was the Vatican. It was open to the public, unlike many of the libraries of the

Middle Ages. Now libraries were open to everyone instead of to just a small number of wealthy or religious collectors.

During the sixteenth century, libraries were built in almost every major European city.

Reading benches were placed close to bookshelves, and valuable volumes were chained to the shelves. Each chain was three to four feet long, with a ring at either end. One ring was attached to the shelf; the other to the cover of the book so that it wouldn't be stolen.

When Henry VIII introduced the Protestant religion to England in the 1600s, many fine Catholic libraries were destroyed. But a large number of new libraries took their place.

In the eighteenth century, when people were interested in science, libraries became important centers of learning and research. On January 15, 1759 the British Museum, which housed a huge national library, was opened in London.

During the French Revolution (1789–1801), many private libraries were donated to the Bibliothèque Nationale in Paris, making it one of the largest libraries in Europe.

In America, the early settlers had small private libraries. Most of their books were on religion, but there were also titles on history and travel as well as a few classics.

In the 1800s, pioneers traveling west took some books with them. But because they had to work hard and money was scarce, their collections were small.

It wasn't until the nineteenth century that people became interested in a "public library."

After 1850, when people had more wealth and leisure time, public libraries were built in cities and towns all over America.

The Main Reading Room
at the Library of Congress
Washington, D.C.

Some of the most beautiful reading rooms in the world are in the Library of Congress in Washington, D.C., America's largest library.

Founded in 1800, the library suffered through two great fires that almost destroyed its collection.

In both cases, the collection was rebuilt with donations and purchases.

The Library of Congress contains all the documents of Congress, papers from the American Revolution, and the private collections of Thomas Jefferson, Benjamin Franklin, Alexander Hamilton, and others.

It also houses a large collection of Chinese, Slavic, and Hispanic literature, as well as newspapers, musical scores, movies, prints, maps, and photographs. Copyrights for inventions, books, and music are filed there and it contains the national library for the blind.

The Library of Congress is a center of culture for our nation.

At hospitals, libraries even come to one's bedside to bring good cheer.

Libraries, then, are wonderful places. They are open to all people, and they have books for all ages and on all subjects.

At hospitals, they even come to one's bedside to bring good cheer. So, hooray for libraries and hooray for books!

MORE · ABOUT · LIBRARIES

To borrow a book from the library, you need a library card. To get one, simply go to the main desk and ask what you should do next.

The great artist Michelangelo designed the Laurentian Library in Florence, Italy, which opened its doors in 1525.

Benjamin Franklin helped to start one of the first libraries from which one could borrow books, in 1732. It was called the Library Company of Philadelphia.

The Library of Congress has approximately 550 miles of bookshelves.

The largest library in the world is the Lenin Memorial Library in Moscow, founded in the eighteenth century.

The New York Public Library was opened in 1911. Two proud and friendly lion sculptures greet visitors at its entrance. Named Fortitude and Patience, they wear wreaths around their necks at Christmas.

Index